REVOLUTIONARY PRUDENCE WRIGHT

Leading *the* Minute Women
in the Fight for Independence

Beth Anderson

Illustrated by Susan Reagan

CALKINS CREEK

AN IMPRINT OF ASTRA BOOKS FOR YOUNG READERS

New York

A Love Box

"These are the times that try men's ^and women's *souls."*

—Thomas Paine

Prudence Cummings painted, snipped, and folded her precious piece of paper, crafting a "love box" like any colonial girl.

But when she bested boys at school,

hunted and fished with her father,

and debated her brothers on the rule of the British King, it was clear . . . Prudence had a spark of independence.

Year after year, Prudence fumed as King George III of England tightened his grip on the American colonies. He robbed them of hard-earned money with taxes on tea, sugar, glass, paper, lead, and paint. He denied their rights to make their own laws and sell their own goods. He invaded their homes with British soldiers who demanded free room and board.

Tensions mounted as suspicion crept among the colonists . . .

Who was a Tory, loyal to the King?

Who was a patriot, determined to fight for their rights?

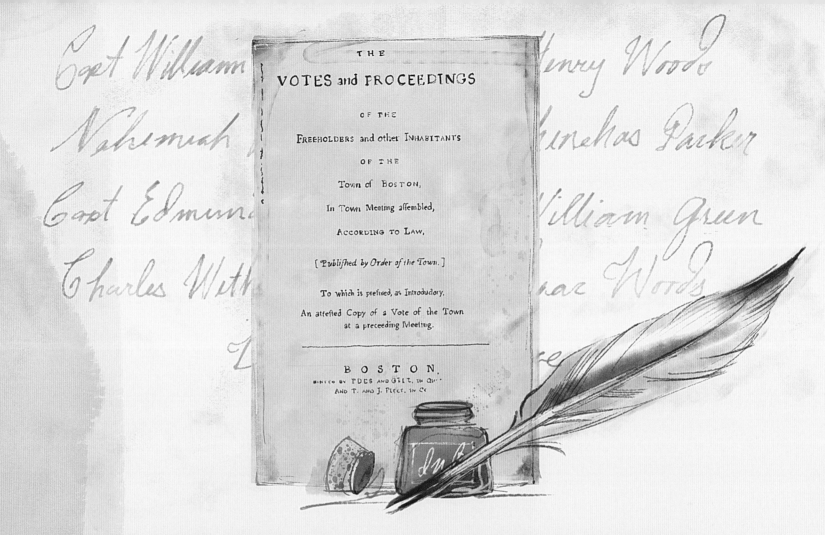

In January 1773, Prudence and her husband David packed into the meeting house with the citizens of Pepperell. A new pamphlet had arrived from patriot leaders in Boston. The restless crowd quieted, anxious to hear every word . . .

Rights of the colonists!

Violations by the King!

Were the towns willing to join the fight?

Male voices rose in a chorus of "Ayes." It was unanimous.

With signatures inked on paper, Pepperell, Massachusetts, officially joined the network of resistance. A network that stretched from Boston to meeting houses across the colony and into homes.

Prudence and the women sewed scraps of cloth into quilts. When talk turned to the possibility of war, her stitches lurched out of line. Ripping them back, straightening them out, she studied the quilt— small pieces, repeating patterns. She scanned the circle of women. Small actions, too, might form a pattern—a pattern of rebellion.

Inspired by the patriots in Boston who protested the King's tax on tea, the women brewed a plan of their own.

They marched from their homes, dumped their tea on the town common, and set it aflame.

No British tea! Prudence grew herbs and made her own Liberty Tea.

No British cloth! She spun flax into linen and wove homespun fabric.

No British sugar! She boiled maple sap into syrup.

No gloves or garments, no ribbons or buttons, no glass or paper! She would do without. Prudence could live with inconvenience and additional work. But she couldn't live with unjust laws and stolen rights.

The pattern of rebellion grew.

BY THE

KING

A

PROCLAMATION,

Act to discontinue, in such Manner and for such Time as are therein mentioned, the landing and discharging, lading or shipping, of Goods, Wares, and Merchandise at the Town, and within the Harbour, of the Province of Massachuset's Bay in America.

The King struck back.
He outlawed town meetings,
closed the port in Boston,
and sent ships with more troops.

The patriots prepared for war.
They formed their own government, organized alarm riders to warn of British troop movements, and armed town militias—minutemen—ready to fight at a moment's notice.

While David trained on the common with the men, Prudence molded bullets at home, hoping they'd never be used.

Prudence and David cheered as Pepperell raised a liberty flag in defiance of the King.

But not everyone in the colonies united against British rule. If it came to war, the conflict between patriots and Tories would rip Prudence's family apart.

Heading north to visit her mother, Prudence wondered how far her Tory brothers would go in this fight. Would she be forced to choose between family and freedom?

As she chatted with her mother, Prudence heard voices in the next room. Peering around the corner, she spied an old schoolmate, Leonard Whiting, and her brother Samuel. She caught a word here and there. *Messages. Troops. The British. Boston.* Samuel! Her favorite brother—a spy?

Prudence slipped out and hurried home.

Days later, as Prudence's family slept, horsemen raced from Boston to Lexington to Concord . . . horse hooves pounded through the moonlit night . . . across the countryside . . . raising the alarm. By morning, a rider reached Pepperell to warn of advancing British troops. "The Regulars are coming!"

David ran from the field, grabbed his coat and musket, and rushed
to the alarm post. The commander issued orders, and Pepperell's
minutemen marched off to battle.

Prudence held her five children close, wondering if she'd ever see
her husband again. Then she grabbed the plow and picked up where
David left off. The women of Pepperell became farmers, blacksmiths,
merchants, and millers.

The next day, couriers brought news of patriots pushing the redcoats back to Boston.

Then came reports of dead and wounded.

Soon rumors raced across the countryside. *The redcoats are coming! Invading towns! Ransacking homes! Burning shops! Tory spies!*

Some people fled, but Prudence remained. She knew no one was watching the bridge in Pepperell, a main route for the British between Canada and Boston. She knew spies and messengers could pass unnoticed. And she knew if British troops came through, the minute-men would be trapped.

Prudence ran from neighbor to neighbor. Within minutes, women emerged from their homes dressed in the clothes of husbands, fathers, brothers, and sons. More and more joined as they flowed down the street carrying old muskets, pitchforks, axes, shovels, whatever they could find.

The women weren't organized and trained like the men, but they were bound together, like blocks of a quilt. The first-ever unit of minute women assembled at the bridge and elected Prudence their leader.

Captain Prudence surveyed the road winding around the hill.
British troops or messengers would come from the north. The
bridge would remain unseen until the last minute.

Prudence shielded her lantern, and the women settled into the
shadows to wait.

As darkness deepened, so did their worry. How many would they face?
How long could they hide their identity? What if they were captured . . . or worse?

Horses.
From the north.
Prudence issued orders and hushed the women.
She listened.
How many?
One?
Two?
Prudence peered into the night.

Nearing the bridge, the hoofbeats slowed, then started across the wooden planks.

Halt! The minute women leaped out of the shadows as Prudence's voice cut through the darkness.

The second horseman spun around.

But Prudence caught a glimpse.

Her brother Samuel raced away.

The women surrounded the remaining rider and seized the reins.

Just as Prudence had suspected—Captain Leonard Whiting, loyal to the King.

Whiting studied the faces behind pitchforks and axes. Women?

They snatched his gun.

His eyes widened. Prudence! Not the schoolgirl he remembered. But the same independent spirit.

She ordered him to dismount and began the search.

Hat,

coat,

boots . . .

Aha! She reached into his boot, pulled out a wad of papers, and unfolded them.

Dispatches for British troops!

They had caught their spy!

The women bound their prisoner, marched him to a
nearby tavern, and guarded him overnight. In the morning,
they delivered Whiting and the papers to patriot authorities.

When the men returned home with tales of their battles, the women listened. Then wives, mothers, sisters, and daughters shared a story of their own—of Captain Prudence Wright, the minute women of Pepperell, and the capture of a Tory spy.

Prudence passed down many treasures to the generations that followed: her paper "love box," her quilts, the lantern she carried that night. But the greatest of all is her story—a bridge connecting us to the past and the dawn of a revolution. When Prudence Cummings Wright and the minute women of Pepperell marched from their homes and took up "arms" against the British, they did much more than declare independence from the King's rule. They broke free from traditional female roles, never surrendered to fear, and proved themselves as full citizens. Revolutionary women, indeed!

Afterword

One hundred and ten years after her ancestors came to America, Prudence Cummings was born on November 26, 1740, in what would soon become Hollis, New Hampshire.

As a child, she did what was expected of every colonial girl: knit socks, sewed patchwork quilts, stitched a sampler, and completed her church catechism. Prudence performed her chores to perfection, earning rewards from her parents such as playtime or a sheet of paper. One precious piece of paper became her "love box" and still exists today.

Unlike most girls of her time, Prudence also attended school, hunted and fished, and participated in family discussions of politics.

As Prudence grew, she became proficient at spinning, dyeing, and weaving. She molded candles, bullets, and pewter spoons. She knew how to handle a flintlock, spear, fishing line, snowshoes, and horse. With her mother, she made cheese and butter, cured meat, and cooked. Prudence became well-known for her sand-scouring designs, creating art as she used sand to clean the floor. She was also a respected quilt designer and painter.

During her childhood, Prudence enjoyed fine British goods her father brought from Boston: silk, lace, ribbons, gloves, shoes, and fancy cloth. But by the time she married David Wright of Pepperell, Massachusetts, in 1761, life had become more difficult due to the rule of King George III of England.

As the King imposed more taxes and restrictions, the colonists were faced with the choice of continuing to obey him just because he was the King, or risking the consequences of pushing back against his policies. Their resentment of "taxation without representation" led to boycotts, and eventually rebellion.

Prudence, feisty and fearless, led the women of Pepperell in defiance of the King. Refusing British goods created a tightly knit community but resulted in more work for every member of the family.

A few days after April 19, 1775, when the men left for Concord, Prudence rallied the women. She walked several miles to the bridge that night where thirty to forty minute women assembled. If they hadn't disarmed Leonard Whiting before he realized he'd been stopped by a group of women, the ending might have been different.

In 1777, the town of Pepperell recognized the minute women for capturing Leonard Whiting at the bridge. Unable to pay women for patriotic service, the town issued payment of seven pounds, seventeen shillings, and six pence to "Leonard Whiting's Guard." The money went to the women and the tavern owner who accommodated them overnight.

While Prudence's youngest brother, Benjamin, fought with the minutemen of Hollis, it's unlikely she ever saw her two Tory brothers, Samuel and Thomas, after the bridge incident. In 1776, Samuel and Thomas Cummings, along with Leonard Whiting and his brother Benjamin, were summoned by patriot authorities as "Suspected Persons of being unfriendly or Enemicall to the Libertys and rights of the United Colonys." They were soon released due to insufficient evidence. But Thomas was called back. After posting bail, he left the country. Samuel Cummings and Benjamin Whiting also fled.

There are no records of Leonard Whiting's detention after being captured at the bridge or of the papers he carried. Most likely, he claimed he was a British officer following orders. Records show Leonard Whiting served jail time in 1777–78. After release, he moved to Vermont and became an upright citizen.

Prudence Cummings Wright, guardian of the bridge, died in Pepperell at age 84 on December 2, 1824.

Today, a granite tablet stands near the bridge, reminding all who pass of Prudence Cummings Wright and the minute women of Pepperell. The town continues to celebrate these women who, with men away at battle and children asleep in their beds, mustered their courage at a moment's notice and guarded the bridge in defense of freedom.

Author's Research Note

The greatest challenge in telling Prudence Cummings (also spelled Cumings) Wright's story is an incomplete historical record. Local and genealogical records list dates of births and deaths, but little more. (Records are inconsistent about her date of death, but experts believe that 1824 is correct.) Town meeting notes reveal small bits and pieces, such as the raising of the Liberty flag and payment of the women. There are no written accounts of the event at the bridge until 1848, seventy-three years after it happened, time enough for memories to fade. The history of Groton states that Leonard Whiting was captured with "despatches [sic] from Canada to the British in Boston," and that he and the papers were turned over to patriot authorities.

The more personal accounts of the story have been handed down through oral history and were recorded in 1899 by Mary Shattuck. She shares three versions which differ on a few details. The "grandmothers" reported that Prudence visited her mother's home for a few days in March after the death of her baby. A descendant of Prudence adds to this, claiming that when she visited her mother, she overheard her brother Samuel and Leonard Whiting talking about leading British forces to Groton, just south of the bridge. In this version, both men were captured, and Samuel, recognizing his sister's voice, told Whiting to lower his gun as his sister would "wade through blood for the rebel cause." The third variation is from a descendant of Leonard Whiting. This one says that as two riders approached the bridge, they heard the women's voices. Prudence's brother Thomas recognized his sister's voice and fled while Whiting continued across the bridge.

In addition, it's not clear whether the women had established a rotating guard unit that patrolled the streets and bridge over several days or whether rumors inspired them to rush to the bridge that night.

As with many historical events, the research leaves us with unanswered questions. Some might also wonder if Prudence's choice that night changed history. After reading all the research and corresponding with a few of today's women of Pepperell, the answer is yes. Even though we're not able to evaluate the military significance of her actions, there's no doubt that she emboldened the women of her time to break free of tradition and participate more fully in society. Not only that, her story continues to inspire us today.

Illustrator's Note

I knew illustrating a book about thirty women would be a challenge. I wanted to depict their bravery, but also their vulnerability—I would have been so scared on that bridge! Prudence was a mother and a wife, informed, opinionated, stubborn, and my favorite, a fellow artist. So, the challenge was to create historically accurate illustrations that captured the range of emotion, conveyed the drama and chaos of the night, and, at the end, reflected the future of women in society—hence the image of all the women of Pepperell standing arm in arm.

This is my first historical picture book and the research and attention to detail involved enthralled me. But a pandemic hit, so my Pepperell road trip to photograph the countryside and visit historical sites was off. I learned that finding references from the 1700s is not always easy. Thankfully, there are historical paintings, war reenactments, and the wonderful author and experts who provided images of Prudence's lantern and love box. One image we couldn't find was the "Liberty Flag," which explains why only a tip of the flag is visible when the town of Pepperell raises it. The bridge was also an educated guess, since the original bridge was damaged in a flood in 1818 and replaced by a covered bridge. Adding illustrations of historical documents and recreating them in my hand lettering became a fun design element that added context. Type in the 1770s was usually pretty wonky and typesetting was not a perfect business, which inspired me to keep my hand lettering rugged and textural. My artwork combines traditional watercolor painting with digital drawing in order to evoke images from the past.

Bibliography

Primary Sources

"Meeting of the Inhabitants of the District of Pepperell, January 11, 1773." Pepperell, MA—official website. town.pepperell.ma.us/146/Revolutionary-War—1.

"News of the Beginning of the American Revolution." Pepperell, MA—official website. town.pepperell.ma.us/149/Revolutionary-War—4.

"Resolutions by the Inhabitants of the District of Pepperell, June 27, 1774." Pepperell, MA—official website. town.pepperell.ma.us/147/Revolutionary-War—2.

"Town Meeting Dated: August 29, 1774." Pepperell, MA—official website. town.pepperell.ma.us/148/Revolutionary-War—3.

"Town Meeting Dated: March 19, 1777." Pepperell, MA—official website. town.pepperell.ma.us/150/Revolutionary-War—5.

Secondary Sources

"Amazonian Patriots." *Boston Sunday Globe*, April 19, 1896, vol. XLIX, no. 110.

Bouton, Nathaniel, D. D., ed. *Documents and Records Relating to the State of New-Hampshire During the Period of the American Revolution from 1776 to 1783.* Vol. 8. Concord, NH: Edward A. Jenks, State Printer, 1874. 156.

Brown, Richard D. "Massachusetts Towns Reply to the Boston Committee of Correspondence, 1773." *The William and Mary Quarterly* 25, no. 1 (1968): 22–39.

Butler, Caleb. *History of the Town of Groton, including Pepperell and Shirley, from the First Grant of Groton Plantation in 1655.* Boston: T. R. Marvin, 1848. 335–37.

Cummins, Albert Orin. *Cummings Genealogy: Isaac Cummings, 1601–1677 of Ipswich in 1638 and Some of His Descendants.* Montpelier, VT: Argus and Patriot Printing House, 1904. 44–46.

Drake, Samuel Adams, ed. *History of Middlesex County, Massachusetts: Containing Carefully Prepared Histories of Every City and Town in the County.* Vol. 2. Boston: Estes and Lauriat, 1880. 263.

Fischer, David Hackett. *Paul Revere's Ride.* Oxford University Press, 1994.

Frank, Lisa Tendrich, ed. *An Encyclopedia of American Women at War: From the Home Front to the Battlefields.* Vol. 1. Santa Barbara, CA: ABC-CLIO, 2013. 669–70.

Green, Harry Clinton, and Mary Wolcott Green. "IV. Daring and Devotion of the Women of '76." *The Pioneer Mothers of America: A Record of the More Notable Women of the Early Days of the Country. . . .* Vol. 2. New York: Putnam & Sons, 1912. 316–36.

Hunter, John P. "'No Foe to Freedom Should Pass That Bridge.'" *Colonial Williamsburg* 28, (Summer 2006): 36–41.

"The Late William Wright." *Boston Daily Advertiser,* Aug. 17, 1859, Issue 40: n.p.

Miner, Laurence A. "Prudence Wright." *A Pepperell Reader: Dedicated to the People of Pepperell, past and present.* 1975, reprint courtesy of the Pepperell Historical Society. 53–55.

Mooar, George, comp. *The Cummings Memorial, A Genealogical History of the Descendants of Isaac Cummings, An Early Settler of Topsfield, Massachusetts.* New York: B. F. Cummings, 1903. 49–52.

New England Historic Genealogical Society. *The New England Historical and Genealogical Register for the year 1860.* Vol. 14. Boston: Samuel G. Drake, 1860. 90.

Robbins, Lyman F. "A History of Pepperell." *Pepperell Free Press,* May 28, 1970.

Ryan, D. Michael. *Concord and the Dawn of Revolution: The Hidden Truths.* Charleston, SC: History Press, 2007.

Sabine, Lorenzo. *Biographical Sketches of Loyalists of the American Revolution with an Historical Essay.* Vol. 2. Boston: Little, Brown, 1864. 422–23.

Shattuck, Mary L. P. *Prudence Wright and the Women Who Guarded the Bridge: The Story of Jewett's Bridge.* 1964. Ayer, Mass: H. S. Turner, [1912].

Skemp, Sheila L. "Women and Politics in the Era of the American Revolution." *Oxford Research Encyclopedia of American History.* Oxford University Press, June 9, 2016.

Spaulding, Charles S. "Captain Leonard Whiting." *An Account of Some of the Early Settlers of West Dunstable, Monson and Hollis N.H.* Nashua, NH: Telegraph Press, 1915. 231.

Tinklepaugh, Joan Child. "Eleven: The Cumings Family, The House Divided." *Hollis Family Album: The Folk Tales and Family Trees of the First Settlers of Hollis, New Hampshire, 1730–1950.* Camden, ME: Penobscot, 1997. 215–19.

Worcester, Samuel T. *History of the Town of Hollis, New Hampshire, from Its First Settlement to the Year 1879: With Many Biographical Sketches of Its Early Settlers, Their Descendants, and Other Residents: Illustrated with Maps and Engravings.* Boston: A. Williams, 1879. 160–61.

Wright, Frank V. "The Story of Prudence Wright's Guard as Told by a Family Descendant (reprint)." Letter to Mary Shattuck. Feb. 28, 1900, Salem, MA.

Websites

Bell, J. L. "Arrest at Pepperell Bridge." *Boston 1775* (blog). Aug. 29, 2010. boston1775.blogspot.com/2010/08/arrest-at-pepperell-bridge.html.

———. "'Persons Suspected of Being Inimical.'" *Boston 1775* (blog). Aug. 31, 2010. boston1775.blogspot.com/2010/08/persons-suspected-of-being-inimical.html.

———. "Prudence Wright and Her Brothers." *Boston 1775* (blog). Aug. 30, 2010. boston1775.blogspot.com/2010/08/prudence-wright-and-her-brothers.html.

"Boston Committee of Correspondence Document Known as The "Boston Pamphlet" A. The Rights of the Colonists B. Violations of Those Rights C. A Letter of Correspondence 1772 Excerpts." *Making the Revolution: America 1763–1791 Primary Source Collection, America in Class,* National Humanities Center.

MacLean, Maggie. "Prudence Cummings Wright." *History of American Women* (blog). May 1, 2009. womenhistoryblog.com/2009/05/prudence-cummings-wright.html.

Source Notes

"These are ...": Paine, Thomas. *The American Crisis.* Philadelphia: Styner and Cist, 1776.

"Suspected Persons of being unfriendly ...": Bouton, *Documents and Records Relating to the State of New-Hampshire ...,* p. 156.

"despatches [sic] from Canada to the British in Boston": Butler, *History of the Town of Groton,* p. 336.

"wade through blood ...": Shattuck, *Prudence Wright and the Women Who Guarded the Bridge,* p. 36.

Acknowledgments

Immense thanks to the women of Pepperell, Massachusetts, who provided information and inspired me with their dedication to the story of Prudence Wright: Wendy Cummings, Regent of the Prudence Wright Chapter, National Society Daughters of the American Revolution; Susan Smith, President of Pepperell Historical Society; Diane Cronin, Chairman of Pepperell Historical Commission; and Tina McEvoy, Lawrence Library. Thanks also to Ronald Dale Karr, Pepperell Historical Commission; to the Groton, Hollis, New Hampshire, Massachusetts, and New England historical societies; to the Massachusetts and New Hampshire state archives; and to the Library of Congress and public libraries of Groton, Hollis, Pepperell, and Boston. Much appreciation to all my "encouragers": critique partners Julie, Kristen F., Ann, Kristen O., Michelle, Heather, Maria, and Vivian; my agent Stephanie Fretwell-Hill; editor Carolyn Yoder; and, of course, my family who comes along on these journeys of discovery.

For my daughters, Carla and Lauren —*BA*
For my brave sisters, my best friends —*SR*

For information about permission to reproduce selections from this book, please contact permissions@astrapublishinghouse.com.

Calkins Creek • An imprint of Astra Books for Young Readers, a division of Astra Publishing House • calkinscreekbooks.com

Printed in China

ISBN: 978-1-64472-057-8 (hc) • ISBN: 978-1-63592-556-2 (eBook)
Library of Congress Control Number: 2021906341

First edition
10 9 8 7 6 5 4 3 2 1

Design by Barbara Grzeslo • The text is set in ITC Avant Garde Gothic. • The illustrations are done in watercolor with digital drawing.